Julie's JOURNEY

By MEGAN MCDONALD

ILLUSTRATIONS ROBERT HUNT

VIGNETTES SUSAN MCALILEY

★ AmericanGirl®

THE AMERICAN GIRLS

  KAYA, an adventurous Nez Perce girl whose deep love for horses and respect for nature nourish her spirit

1774  FELICITY, a spunky, spritely colonial girl, full of energy and independence

1824  JOSEFINA, a Hispanic girl whose heart and hopes are as big as the New Mexico sky

1853  CÉCILE AND MARIE-GRACE, two girls whose friendship helps them—and New Orleans—survive terrible times

1854  KIRSTEN, a pioneer girl of strength and spirit who settles on the frontier

1864 · ADDY, a courageous girl determined to be free in the midst of the Civil War

1904 · SAMANTHA, a bright Victorian beauty, an orphan raised by her wealthy grandmother

1914 · REBECCA, a lively girl with dramatic flair growing up in New York City

1934 · KIT, a clever, resourceful girl facing the Great Depression with spirit and determination

1944 · MOLLY, who schemes and dreams on the home front during World War Two

1974 · JULIE, a fun-loving girl from San Francisco who faces big changes—and creates a few of her own

Published by American Girl Publishing

Questions or comments? Call 1-800-845-0005, visit **americangirl.com**,
or write to Customer Service, American Girl, 8400 Fairway Place,
Middleton, WI 53562-0497.

Printed in China
12 13 14 15 16 LEO 12 11 10 9 8 7 6

All American Girl marks, Julie®, and Julie Albright™
are trademarks of American Girl.

PICTURE CREDITS
The following individuals and organizations have generously
given permission to reprint images contained in "Looking Back":
p. 73—courtesy of Sharan and Sherry Bethke; pp. 74–75—© Pat O'Hara/Corbis (barn); photo by
Joe Maerzke/JEM (covered wagon, unloading barges); pp. 76–77—photo by Mike Longworth
(girl on bicycle); © Wally McNamee/Corbis (parade, girl and old woman); © Charles E. Rotkin/
Corbis (tall ship); pp. 78–79—photo by Jim Britt for Time & Life Pictures/Getty images (Time
magazine "Roots" cover); Elsie is a trademark of Borden Foods. Used with permission; Wisconsin
Historical Society (tractor); courtesy of Sharan and Sherry Bethke (children with signs); p. 80—
© Wally McNamee/Corbis (President Ford); photo by Joe Maerzke/JEM (children with flags).

Library of Congress Cataloging-in-Publication Data

McDonald, Megan.
Julie's journey / by Megan McDonald ; illustrations, Robert Hunt ;
vignettes, Susan McAliley.
84 p. : ill. ; 22 cm.
Summary: It's 1976 and the entire country is celebrating America's 200th birthday. Julie joins her
cousins on a pioneer-style wagon train in honor of the Bicentennial. The journey is filled with
adventures, challenges, and self-discovery as Julie faces her fears to make an important contribution
to her country's birthday. The "Looking Back" section provides additional information about
Bicentennial celebrations in the United States.—from publisher's description.
ISBN 978-1-59369-352-7 (pbk.: alk. paper) — ISBN 978-1-59369-353-4 (hardcover: alk. paper)
[1. American Revolution Bicentennial, 1976—Juvenile fiction. 2. Wagon trains—Juvenile fiction.
3. Family—California—San Francisco—Juvenile fiction. 4. American Revolution Bicentennial,
1976—Fiction. 5. Wagon trains—Fiction. 6. Family life—Fiction. 7. San Francisco (Calif.)—History—
20th century—Juvenile fiction. 8. San Francisco (Calif.)—History—20th century—Fiction.]
I. Hunt, Robert, 1952–, ill. II. McAliley, Susan, ill. III. Title.
[Fic]—dc22   2007280650

FOR REGINA SHIPMAN HAYNES

Table of Contents

Julie's Journey

Julie's Family

JULIE
*A girl full of energy
and new ideas, trying to
find her place in
times of change*

TRACY
*Julie's trendy
teenage sister, who is
sixteen years old*

MOM
*Julie's artistic
mother, who runs
a small store*

DAD
*Julie's father,
an airline pilot who flies
all over the world*

IVY
*Julie's best friend,
who loves doing
gymnastics*

APRIL
*Julie's cousin, who is
thirteen and knows how
to ride horses*

Julie Albright lifted her long calico dress to lace up her shoes, smoothed her apron, and tied the strings of her sunbonnet. "How do I look?"

"Like a real pioneer," said Mom, taking straight pins from between her lips. "I have to finish off this hem. Dad'll be here to pick you girls up first thing in the morning."

As Mom pinned up the hem of the pioneer dress, Julie hugged herself with excitement. Tomorrow Dad was taking Tracy and her to the airport for their very first trip on an airplane. They were flying east to Pittsburgh, where Julie and Tracy would join their Aunt Catherine, Uncle Buddy, and cousins Jimmy and April to celebrate the Fourth of July.

But this was not just any July Fourth celebration, Julie reminded herself. It was the Bicentennial, and Julie and her sister were going to be part of a very special event. An old-fashioned pioneer-style wagon train, with wagons from all fifty states, was crossing the country in honor of America's two-hundredth birthday. Except unlike the pioneer days, this wagon train was starting on the West Coast and heading *east*, all the way to Pennsylvania. "It's like history in reverse," Dad had put it. In Pittsburgh, Julie and Tracy would join their cousins on a horse-drawn wagon for the last three weeks of the journey.

Julie shivered with anticipation. An airplane. . . *and* a covered wagon! She would be like Laura Ingalls Wilder, who had crossed the prairie with her family in the Little House books. Julie could hardly wait.

Tracy stopped brushing her hair and held up the green and white cotton dress Mom had made for her. "Did pioneers really wear these long dresses and ugly aprons? I'll die of embarrassment if I have to wear this. I look like Raggedy Ann."

"You can wear blue jeans on the wagon," said Mom. "But take the dress—you may want to wear it when you get to Valley Forge."

"Think of it as dressing up for a big giant birthday party for our whole country," Julie said with enthusiasm. "Just think, two hundred years ago was the *original* Fourth of July, with the Declaration of Independence." Julie held up a hairbrush in a dramatic pose. "Give me liberty or give me death!"

"Give *me* my hairbrush," said Tracy, grabbing the brush and stuffing it into her overflowing suitcase. "Okay, I'll take the dress, but I need a second suitcase. I haven't even packed my pillow yet, or my magazines, or—"

"Why not take your tennis racket, and your hair dryer, and your princess phone?" Julie asked, turning to admire her pioneer outfit in the mirror.

"Ha, ha, Julie Ingalls Wilder," Tracy teased back.

Mom smiled. "I sure am going to miss you girls," she sighed, handing each of them a gift.

Julie unwrapped her present. Inside was a blank book covered in fabric with orange pop-art daisies. "A journal!" She hugged the book to her. "Thanks, Mom. It's perfect."

"A trip like this is a once-in-a-lifetime event," said Mom. "You'll want to remember everything that happens."

Julie finished packing. It didn't take long—from all the weekends she'd spent at Dad's house, she'd become an expert packer. She neatly tucked her pioneer dress on top of her jeans, her T-shirts, and her Little House books.

"Please tell me you're not taking all nine of those books in your suitcase," said Tracy.

"Why not? At least my stuff all *fits* in one suitcase." Julie glanced at Tracy's two bulging suitcases. "Looks like you're taking your whole closet and half the bathroom."

Tracy shrugged. "So? *Anything* could happen on this trip. This way I'll be prepared no matter what."

That night, a fluttery mixture of excitement and nervousness kept Julie from falling asleep. She opened her new journal to the first page and wrote:

Things I want to do on my trip:

Ride a horse

Learn pioneer stuff like building a fire
Sleep in a tent
Make friends with cousin April

Julie paused and chewed the end of her pencil. There was something else she wanted to add, but she didn't know quite how to put it. Finally she wrote:

Do something special for my country.

She read over her list. The last line looked a little funny. After all, the wagon train was something special. Maybe that was enough. But Julie couldn't help hoping that somehow she could do more than just go along for the ride. She remembered last spring, when she had helped a wildlife rescue center raise money to release a family of bald eagles back into the wild. Watching those eagles finally soaring free had been more thrilling than any fireworks on the Fourth of July. Just thinking about it made Julie shiver with happiness.

The wagon train journey would be a once-in-a-lifetime event, as Mom had said. Julie hoped that somehow, she could be a special part of it.

"Buckle up," said Julie's father. "We're getting ready for takeoff."

Julie looked out the window as the 707 pulled away from the terminal. "This is so boss! Is it hard to drive one of these things, Dad?"

"Not if you know how." Julie's father smiled. "If you think this is fun, just wait until we're 27,000 feet above the earth."

Julie looked at her sister with excitement, but Tracy sat stiffly, facing forward and gripping the armrests of her seat.

"Just relax, honey. Flying's even safer than

riding in a car," Dad reassured her.

"But in a car, the wheels never leave the ground," Tracy muttered. As the plane started to taxi down the runway, picking up speed, she reached over and gripped Dad's hand.

"Close your eyes," Dad softly encouraged. "Take a deep breath."

Soon they were high up in the air. The sky was the brightest blue Julie had ever seen, and the plane hovered over pillows of cotton-candy clouds. "Tracy, look! I can see the Golden Gate Bridge. And there are teeny little cars that look like toys."

Tracy glanced out the window and then sank back in her seat, looking a bit green. But her face lit up when Dad handed her a set of headphones and showed her how to tune in the music channels.

Dad took out a map of Pennsylvania and spread it across Julie's tray table. Julie traced her finger along the route Dad had highlighted. It ended at Valley Forge.

"Dad, how come all the wagons are going to Valley Forge?" Julie asked.

"Well, it's a big park, so there'll be enough space for all the wagons, horses, and people," said Dad.

"And two hundred years ago, George Washington and his soldiers spent a long, hard winter in Valley Forge during the Revolutionary War. So it's an important place in history."

"Yeah, they were freezing and starving," Tracy chimed in. "We read about it in school. They didn't have enough shoes, or coats, or food, or anything. A lot of soldiers got sick." She shook her head. "I never would have made it, that's for sure."

Dad chuckled. "Even those soldiers barely made it, but in the end, they pulled through—and turned the tide of the war. And because of them, we're here today, and our country is two hundred years old."

Julie thought back to that winter so long ago. It was difficult imagining the hardships those soldiers had lived through—and all because they had this idea of starting a new country. Would she be willing to go through that, all for an idea that might not even work? And later, settlers crossing the country in horse-drawn wagons to find new homes had known hunger and sickness, too. Julie looked out the airplane window into the vast blue sky. It was strange to think about George Washington and his soldiers, pioneers like Laura

Ingalls and her family, and now her *own* family flying through the air in a jet plane—and how they were all part of the same country. They were all connected.

CHAPTER TWO

WAGONS, HO!

It was still dark the next morning when Julie, Tracy, and Dad headed out of the city to meet their cousins at the crack of dawn. They crossed a long bridge, leaving the glittering lights of Pittsburgh behind them.

"No more cities for a while," Dad said. "From now on, it'll be back roads, farmland, and mountains."

"Do you think April will like me?" Julie could barely remember her cousin, whom she hadn't seen since she was five. "I wonder if she likes the Little House books. Do you think she'll have a pioneer dress, too?" Or would April think it was embarrassing, the way Tracy did?

"I think she'll like you much better if you're not such a Chatty Cathy at five o'clock in the morning," Tracy grumbled. Chatty Cathy was a doll that talked and talked when you pulled her string. Julie knew Tracy was teasing her. But she couldn't help smiling, knowing that Tracy would have to get up early *every* morning on the wagon train!

As the sun rose, Julie climbed out of the car near the boat dock and gazed at the strange flotilla slicing through the early morning fog on the river. A tugboat pushing two long barges headed toward the dock. Each barge carried rows of pioneer-style wagons with big white canvas covers. In a silent parade, the wagons came to shore. Throngs of people had gathered at the dock and teams of horses stood patiently, waiting to be hitched up.

"Julie! Tracy! Uncle Dan! Over here!" A long-legged girl with brown hair, bangs, and dimples waved her arms. "It's me, April!" Behind her, Julie recognized Aunt Catherine, Uncle Buddy, and her cousin Jimmy. They all hurried over, engulfing Julie,

Tracy, and Dad in a sea of hugs.

Dad stepped back and took a good look at his niece and nephew. "April, I can't believe you're already thirteen. And look at those sideburns on Jimmy." Jimmy grinned, blushing pink to the roots of his collar-length, wavy brown hair. He was eighteen.

"Don't you think he looks kind of like Pa from *Little House on the Prairie*?" asked April. "That's my all-time favorite TV show."

"Hey, those are my favorite books!" said Julie.

"She brought the whole set with her." Tracy rolled her eyes.

"That's why I can't wait to ride in a real covered wagon," Julie said. "Sometimes Laura used to ride the wagon horses to get water. Do you think I can try riding a horse?"

"You've never ridden a horse before?" April said, sounding surprised. "Wait till you meet Jimmy's horse, Hurricane."

It was Julie's turn to be surprised. She looked at Jimmy. "You have your own horse?"

Jimmy nodded proudly. "Took me four years to save up for him."

"April's a good rider, too," said Aunt Catherine.

"I'm sure she'd be happy to teach you to ride, Julie."

"I'm off to get my instructions," Jimmy announced. "See you all at camp tonight!"

"Jimmy volunteered to be one of the outriders," Uncle Buddy told them. "They make sure the cars don't interfere with the horses on the road, things like that." As Jimmy headed off, he stopped to shake hands with a man dressed in overalls. "Hey, there's Tom Sweeney," said Uncle Buddy. "Tom! Come say hello," he called. "We have two newcomers joining our wagon."

"Mr. Sweeney's our neighbor—he owns the farm next to ours," Aunt Catherine explained. "He's the history buff who got us going on this trip. It's his wagon and horses we're using."

Mr. Sweeney came over and shook hands with Dad, Julie, and Tracy. "So you're the city folks. Pleased to have you join us on the trail," said Mr. Sweeney, flashing a bright smile from within a tanned, leathery face.

"It's my girls who are joining you," Dad said. "I'm just here to see them off."

"In that case, have you signed the rededication pledge yet?" Mr. Sweeney unrolled a long piece of paper. Across the top, in fancy calligraphy, it read "Pledge of Rededication." Below was a quote from the Declaration of Independence, with columns of blank lines for signatures.

"By signing this pledge, people are saying they still believe in the principles our country was founded on—freedom and equality, just like it says in the Declaration of Independence," said Mr. Sweeney. "Millions of people have already signed, and we're collecting the signed scrolls as we roll across the country. At Valley Forge we'll present them to the president. He'll sign one, too."

"*The* president?" asked Tracy. "As in President Ford?"

Mr. Sweeney grinned. "That's the one."

Dad gave a low whistle. "You girls may get to see the president," he said.

Mr. Sweeney went on. "At every town we stop in, people bring us signed scrolls to take to Valley Forge. Would you girls like to help me collect them?"

Julie and April nodded. "I know how to collect signatures," said Julie. "I had my own petition for our school basketball team."

"Great. I'll be glad to have more help," said

14

Mr. Sweeney. "Now, go ahead and sign your own names, if you like." He held out the scroll and offered Dad a pen.

Dad and Tracy signed their names and passed the scroll to Julie. The fancy writing at the top made the scroll look very important. Under the title it said:

> To commemorate this nation's Bicentennial we hereby dedicate ourselves anew to the precepts of our Founding Fathers: We hold these truths to be self-evident, that all men are created equal...

Julie wrote her name on the scroll, using her best cursive. It gave her a chill to sign her name to the pledge, along with millions of other Americans. *I'm making history*, she thought.

At the dock, the wagons were being rolled off the barges one by one. A short, stocky man wearing a badge announced, "Alaska!" as the first official state wagon rolled down the ramp. A hearty cheer rang through the crowd as each wagon was eased off the barge.

"That's Mr. Wescott, the wagon master," April told Julie. "Come on, let's go see our wagon." She led Julie over to her parents, who were harnessing two heavy brown workhorses.

Uncle Buddy looked up. "Meet Mack and Molly, two of the finest Belgian draft horses in Pennsylvania."

Julie held out a hand to Molly, who nuzzled her with a soft snuffle. Suddenly Molly lifted her head, ears pricked forward, and Julie heard thundering hoofbeats. Looking up, she saw Jimmy riding high atop a tall brown and white paint. Julie backed up as the paint sniffed noses with Mack and Molly and then squealed, tossing his head and prancing sideways. Julie didn't know if it was Hurricane's sheer size or his energy that startled her more. Sucking in a short breath, she could feel the drumbeat of her own heart pounding inside her chest.

"Easy, boy," said Aunt Catherine, reaching up to stroke Hurricane's head and neck. She winked at Julie. "He knows he's a beauty."

Julie smiled thinly. She'd been counting the days till she could ride a horse, but now, at the thought of getting on such a mountain of a creature, her knees weakened.

"Don't mind him," said Jimmy, motioning to

Julie to come closer. "He's just excited. Go ahead, you can pet him."

Nervously, Julie reached up to pet the horse on the neck. Hurricane let out a low nicker, and Julie snatched back her hand.

Jimmy chuckled. "That means he likes you."

Suddenly the wagon master's voice rose above the hubbub. "Wagons, ho!" he called. "Load 'em up and moooooove 'em out!"

"Time to go," called Uncle Buddy, buckling one of Mack's harness straps.

"Have a great time," said Dad, hugging his daughters good-bye.

"I wish you were coming too, Dad," Julie said as she and Tracy hugged him back.

"I know, honey. I can't take the time off. But I'll fly the Philadelphia route so that I can meet up with you for the Fourth of July." Dad helped Julie and Tracy up into the wagon.

The wagon had new paint and a warm barn smell. It was crammed full of suitcases, sleeping bags, blankets, food, camping gear, a toolbox, and a bucket of horse brushes. Julie and April accidentally elbowed each other and then broke into giggles as

Julie made her way back to sit down on top of a blanket.

"I can barely stand up in here," said Tracy, touching the inside of the white canvas cover with her hand. "This whole wagon's not much bigger than my canopy bed at home!"

"It reminds me of being inside forts that Jimmy and I used to make with blankets over the kitchen table," April said.

"I think it's cozy," said Julie.

Soon the wagon wheels were creaking and rolling out of the park and onto the dusty road. The girls waved to Dad as he became smaller and smaller, framed by the horseshoe-shaped opening in the canvas at the back of the wagon.

"See you at Valley Forge," Julie called.

Mile after mile, farm after farm, hill after hill, the wagons rolled along past farmhouses, barns, and fields of grazing cows. Perched on a cooler, Julie could see the whole wagon train stretched out behind her like beads on a necklace, disappearing around a curve in the road. There was so much to

"I think it's cozy," said Julie.

19

look at—horses with fancy harnesses and bells on, colorful flags flapping, men in buckskin outfits and Daniel Boone caps, even a dressed-up couple in a wagon that said *Just Married*. Bringing up the rear was an old green station wagon with an American flag on its antenna.

Soon Julie noticed that she could feel every rock and rut in the road under the wagon's wooden wheels. "It's so bumpy, I think my bones are being rearranged," she remarked.

April nodded. "You get used to it after a while."

"In a few days, I bet you'll forget what it's like to ride in a car," Uncle Buddy joked.

At last it was time to stop for lunch. The wagons pulled off the road into a park outside a small town. Children who had been playing in the park gathered nearby, pointing and watching with wide eyes. April nudged Julie as they climbed out of the wagon, saying, "I bet those kids wish they were riding with us!" Julie nodded, proud to be part of such an unusual and important happening.

"I'm so hungry, I could eat a horse," said Uncle Buddy as Aunt Catherine passed out sandwiches.

"Don't say that, Dad—Mack and Molly can hear you!" April laughed.

Julie lay back on the picnic blanket, relieved to have a rest from the bumpy wagon. "This is the best tuna sandwich I've ever had," she announced.

Aunt Catherine smiled. "Food always tastes better on the trail."

A short, stocky man approached. From his badge, Julie recognized him as the wagon master. He shook hands with Uncle Buddy. "Tom Sweeney tells me you have two new wagoneers," he said.

Uncle Buddy introduced Julie and Tracy. "This is Mr. Wescott, our wagon master. He rides in the official Pennsylvania state wagon and leads the way. He's the boss, so make sure you listen to him!" Mr. Wescott winked at the girls.

"I can tell them the rules," said April. "Stay together. Safety first, especially when cars are on the road. And no making money by selling wagon-train souvenirs to people along the way."

Mr. Wescott let out a hearty laugh. "Couldn't have said it better myself. We should make you assistant wagon master. Speaking of souvenirs, I've got to go talk to that fellow." He nodded in the direction of the station wagon with the flag. "He's got a carload of knick-knacks. Some of these folks are becoming quite a nuisance—looking for any way to make a buck, I guess." Waving good-bye, the wagon master headed off.

"That car's been following the wagon train all day," said Jimmy.

Uncle Buddy nodded. "It's a free country, so Mr. Wescott can't stop that fellow from using the roads. All he can do is ban him from selling souvenirs from the wagon train itself."

Julie munched on an apple. "When do we get to help collect scrolls?" she asked.

"In Bakersville, in a few days," said Aunt Catherine. "But right now, you can help me collect paper plates and apple cores."

"Come on, let's go feed the apple cores to Mack and Molly," said April.

When the wagon train finally made camp that night, Julie was so tired, she could barely help April and Tracy pitch the tent they were going to share. But before she turned off her flashlight and went to sleep, she opened her journal and began to write.

June 15

First day on the wagon train. It seemed like we covered a lot of ground, but Jimmy says we went only four miles!

After lunch, I walked right up to Hurricane and fed him an apple core. I don't want April to know I'm a little scared of him. I still want to ride him (I think). Maybe tomorrow.

Tonight Uncle Buddy got out his banjo, and pretty soon we had a fiddle player, two guitars, and a white-haired lady on dulcimer around our campfire. We sang along to "Oh, Susannah" and "She'll Be Comin' Round the Mountain" and ended up laughing more than singing. I felt just like Laura when Pa used to play his fiddle!

Gotta go. April is trying to spy on me and see what I'm writing. I'll get her back—by tickling her to death when she least expects it!

CHAPTER
THREE
—

LIGHTNING
KELLEY

June 18

More wagons join us every day.
This morning April and I counted
forty-one wagons in our wagon train.

Around noon we arrived in the town of Bakersville.
The high school marching band led us through the town,
and hundreds of people lined the streets to cheer us on. It
was sort of a parade. My arm aches from waving so much!

At lunch, we sat near the bandstand in the town
square, where the lady mayor held a special scroll-signing
ceremony. She talked about how her grandmother got
her start when she came from Ireland at the turn of the

century and worked in a cigar factory, making only about five dollars a week. She saved every penny and one day opened her own bakery, and it's still there today.

Then Mr. Sweeney held the scroll as she signed it. When she handed it back to him, I could see tears shining in her eyes. It gave me goose bumps.

As the days passed, Julie settled into the rhythm of life on a wagon train. Each morning, Aunt Catherine made oatmeal and hot chocolate for breakfast. After breakfast, Julie packed up her bedding and helped April and Tracy take down their small tent. While Uncle Buddy harnessed Mack and Molly, the girls helped Aunt Catherine load the wagon. Then they all climbed aboard, waving good-bye to Jimmy as he rode off to join the outriders, and took their place in the line of wagons moving slowly out onto the road.

The June weather was fine and sunny, with a welcome breeze that kept the horses from overheating. The girls usually started out riding with their legs hanging out the back, watching the scenery go by. Sometimes they took turns riding up in front on the buckboard seat with April's parents or walked alongside the wagon to stretch their legs. One afternoon a thunderstorm blew up. The sky darkened, and Aunt Catherine quickly drew the canvas cover closed at both ends. The three girls sat cozily on the floor of the wagon, listening to the rain patter on the canvas cover and giggling about everything and nothing. Julie had never heard anyone laugh as much as her cousin April! Just hearing April giggle made Julie crack up, even when she had no idea what the joke was. And the girls didn't mind the rain. It gave them a chance to play cards and board games and Twenty Questions. The hours slipped by in a rhythm as steady as Mack's and Molly's hoofbeats.

At midday the wagon train usually stopped in a park or field where the horses could graze. While Tracy helped Aunt Catherine prepare lunch, Julie and April liked to wander among the wagons, saying hello to the other people and horses, and each trying to be the first to spot Jimmy and Hurricane. One day they found Jimmy hunched over his saddle, fixing a stirrup strap. Hurricane was tied to a nearby tree.

Jimmy looked up as the girls approached. "April,

would you mind taking Hurricane down to the stream for a drink? He's cooled off now." Jimmy had warned Julie that you couldn't water a horse that was still hot and sweaty—the horse could get sick.

April nodded. "Sure. C'mon, Julie." She untied Hurricane's rope and started across the field toward the creek. Suddenly she turned to Julie. "Hey, want to ride Hurricane? I'll boost you up."

"Really?" Julie's heart began to pound. "But wait. What about a saddle?"

"You can ride bareback," said April. "It's super fun. C'mon, I'll give you a leg up." She cupped her hands to make a foothold. Julie stepped into April's hand and, in one swift motion, swung her other leg up and over the horse.

"Hold on to his mane," April instructed. As April led Hurricane across the grassy field, Julie wobbled from side to side. Hurricane's bare back was slippery. She hunkered down low, clinging to the horse's mane.

"Try to relax," April coached. "Sit up straight and get your balance."

Gradually Julie sat up a little taller, gripping the

27

sides of the horse with her thighs. She eased into the rocking motion of the horse, feeling his warmth against her legs, his back muscles rippling with each step.

"Good—that's it. You're getting it," said April.

"I'm really riding!" said Julie.

"You're doing great! Want to try a trot?" April asked.

"Sure, why not," said Julie.

"Here, take the rope." April tossed the end of the lead rope up to her. Julie let go of the mane with one hand and caught it.

"Now kick him with your heels," April called. She broke into a jog. "Let's go, Hurricane."

Julie swung out her feet and gave the horse a kick. Hurricane shot across the field, heading straight for the creek. *Ba-da-rump, ba-da-rump, ba-da-rump.* All Julie could hear was the beating of hooves and the whoosh of air in her ears. "Help!" she called, but April was fast falling behind.

"*Hangggg onnn!*" April's voice was nearly lost in the thundering of hooves.

Julie clung desperately to Hurricane's side, one leg barely hooked over his back. She clutched at his mane. All she could see was the ground—and Hurricane's pounding hooves. Dust stung her eyes. Her heart thumped against her rib cage. If she fell, surely she'd be trampled.

Just when Julie thought she couldn't hang on another second, Hurricane came to a dead stop at the creek's edge. Julie didn't remember letting go. She didn't remember flying through the air. All she knew was the smack of cold water and the bite of a large rock under her shoulder. The wind was knocked out of her. She took in a ragged breath and scrambled backward on all fours like a crab to get away from Hurricane, who was calmly taking a drink.

"Julie, are you okay?" April asked, helping her to her feet. "Oh no, you're sopping wet. You look like a drowned rat!" She began to giggle.

"It's not funny," said Julie. "I almost got trampled. And after I fell, I could hardly even breathe."

April picked up the lead rope. "You'll be okay. Falling is part of learning to ride. You have to fall at least seven times before you're a good rider."

"Well, forget about learning to ride, then," Julie

muttered. "I'm not getting back up on that horse."

"Oh, don't be such a baby. Look, I won't let go of the rope this time, and we'll just stay at a walk."

"I'm not a baby," said Julie, but her voice came out all wobbly and her legs felt like spaghetti. The girls headed back across the field in silence.

"Hey, Julie, just think—this is kind of like the time in *Little House on the Prairie* when Nellie fell off Laura's horse," said April.

Julie glowered at her cousin. "For your information," she snapped, "that was just in the TV show. The *real* Laura never took Nellie riding—she took her into the stream so that Nellie would get leeches on her legs."

"Leeches? Eeww!" April began to giggle. But this time it didn't make Julie laugh.

June 20, after lunch

I don't care what April or anybody says. I'm not getting back on that horse—ever.

June 20, later

I re-read On the Banks of Plum Creek *for seven whole miles. Translation: I am not talking to April.*

Reading about pioneers is not the same as doing it. Riding Hurricane wasn't like what I imagined. Trying to stay on a bareback horse was harder than turning a cartwheel on the balance beam at gymnastics with Ivy. Maybe it wasn't so hard for Laura when she sat bareback on one of Pa's plow horses, but Hurricane is no plow horse, that's for sure.

Here's what's really bugging me: April thinks she knows all about horses and riding, but she should not have let go of the rope. I could have been hurt. Then she wouldn't have been laughing!

April and Tracy are taking a magazine quiz: are you more like a marshmallow or a carrot? What a dumb question.

I miss Ivy. And Mom. And Dad. And my nice private bedroom with no dumb giggling teenagers.

I never would have made it as a pioneer. Why did I even come on this trip?

At camp that night, Julie helped Uncle Buddy start the cook fire. As she crumpled newspaper for kindling, a picture of an old man holding up a flag caught her eye. "Oldest Man in State Raises Old Glory," the headline said.

"Look at this," she said to Uncle Buddy, showing him the article. "The oldest man in Pennsylvania is a hundred and one years old! His name is Mr. Witherspoon, and he lives in a town called Hershey. It says he hangs his flag out every day."

"A hundred and one? Wow, that's old, all right," said Uncle Buddy.

"Hershey—isn't that where they make Hershey's chocolate bars?" Tracy piped up.

"Yup," said Jimmy, "and we'll be going through Hershey next week. There's a big theme park, and we get to spend a whole day there."

"You'll love Hersheypark," April gushed. "It has great roller coasters, and a skyride, and everything!" Tracy looked excited, but Julie didn't say anything. She loved theme parks, too, but she still wasn't talking to April.

After supper, Tracy and April went into the tent to play a game Tracy had brought called Mystery Date. Julie heard gales of laughter coming out of the glowing tent. She sat alone on a log, poking a stick into the dying embers.

Aunt Catherine came over and sat down beside her. "You were awfully quiet today. Everything okay, honey?" Julie nodded. "You've had a long day. Don't you think you should get to bed?"

"I'm not sleepy," Julie replied. How could she read in the tent, with April and Tracy laughing their heads off?

"That was some fall you took today," Aunt Catherine said gently. "First time's always the worst."

Julie could not keep her lip from quivering. Aunt Catherine put an arm around her and the two sat in the comfort of the quiet dark.

"Have you ever heard the story of Lightning Kelley?" asked her aunt, breaking the silence.

"Who's that?" Julie asked.

"He was your great-great-great-grandfather Elijah Kelley, but everyone called him Lightning."

"Why?" asked Julie. "Was he famous?"

"Sure was, in his day. You've heard of the Pony Express, right? In 1860, that was the fastest way to get mail through the Wild West all the way to California."

"Yeah, we learned about it in school," said Julie, sitting up straighter. "But I never knew that I was related to one of the riders."

"Lightning was only seventeen when he joined up," said Aunt Catherine, "but he could ride a horse like nobody's business. They say he braved robbers, snowstorms, and mountain lions riding for the Pony Express. One time when he was crossing a river, the current was so strong that his horse got swept away right out from under him. He grabbed those saddlebags full of mail, held them high over his head with the river raging all around, and saved the mail. Not a single letter was lost."

"Was his horse okay?" asked Julie.

"Yes, the story goes that he met up with his mustang three miles downriver." Aunt Catherine smiled. "Now, it really is time for bed."

Julie crawled into her sleeping bag, as soft and warm as flannel pajamas. Tracy and April were already asleep. Quietly, Julie flicked on her flashlight and opened her journal one more time.

June 20, nighttime

Lightning Kelley didn't let anything stop him. It's pretty cool to be related to him!

I wonder what he would have thought if he'd seen me

flying off Hurricane and landing in the creek today.

Okay, he probably would have laughed. I suppose it <u>did</u> look sort of funny. But I'm still not going to ride that horse again.

The next morning, Julie slept late. When she emerged from the tent, Tracy was already back from the showers, trying to dry her long hair over the last of the coals from the morning campfire. "How's the shoulder?" she asked.

"Okay, I guess," Julie mumbled, rubbing it. Her shoulder was a little sore, but that wasn't what was bothering her. She took a bite of cold oatmeal.

"Are you still sulking because you fell off that horse?" Tracy asked.

"It's not just that." Julie wanted to tell her sister how let down she felt about the whole trip. She was scared to ride a horse. What was worse, being friends with April felt impossible. But most of all, she was disappointed in herself. She could feel the disappointment making a lump in her throat to go with the lump in her stomach. She pushed the cold oatmeal away.

"You know, Jules, April was just trying to do something nice for you. She knew how much you wanted to ride a horse."

Deep down, Julie knew Tracy was right. But the disappointment wouldn't go away.

For the first hours of the morning, Julie decided to walk. It felt good to move, and the sun was warm on her face. She hiked alongside the docile workhorses. *If only Hurricane had been as quiet as Mack and Molly,* she thought wistfully.

In the afternoon, the wagon train began a long climb uphill. Each wagon went at its own pace. Their own wagon slowed to a snail's crawl, dropping behind the others. After several hours had gone by, Julie peered into the distance. The road dipped and curved around an outcropping of massive rock, but there wasn't another wagon in sight. She couldn't even spot the green station wagon with the flying flag that always followed the wagon train. And they hadn't passed a town all afternoon. There were just rocks, hills, and trees as far as the eye could see. The only sound was the constant buzz-saw humming of cicadas.

Was this how Laura Ingalls had felt crossing the long, lonely, empty prairie? Suddenly Julie missed the familiar honking horns and friendly cable-car bells of San Francisco.

As the shadows grew longer, the hill grew steeper, and Julie could hear Mack and Molly breathing hard as they strained into their collars. Their coats gleamed with sweat. She trudged beside the workhorses, feeling sorry for them.

April poked her head out the front of the wagon. "How much farther do we have to go today?" she asked her parents.

"Mr. Wescott said we have to make it to the top of this mountain by nightfall." Uncle Buddy looked over his shoulder at the setting sun. "I'm guessing it's only a few miles more, if we're lucky."

"But the sun's already going down," said April. "Where's Jimmy? I wish he'd ride back and tell us how much farther we have to go."

Without warning, the wagon lurched hard to the right and jerked to a stop. "Whooaa!" Uncle Buddy called to the horses. He set the brake and jumped down from the leaning wagon.

"Is everybody okay?" Aunt Catherine asked.

"We're okay," said Tracy. "But what happened?"

"Did we hit something?" asked April.

They scrambled down off the wagon. Aunt Catherine shone the flashlight while Uncle Buddy squatted on the ground to check under the right side of the wagon. Julie heard Uncle Buddy catch his breath as the flashlight played over the front wheel. It was stuck in a pothole and bent at an odd angle.

"Is the wheel broken?" April asked.

"I'm not sure," Uncle Buddy said tightly. He crouched lower, peering underneath the wagon. "The wheel seems all right—it's the axle I'm worried about. We'll have to get the wagon up out of this hole so I can take a better look."

"Maybe we could help push," Tracy suggested.

"You read my mind, Trace. Catherine, you drive," said Uncle Buddy. "The rest of us will push."

On the count of three, Aunt Catherine snapped the reins and called out, "Giddap! Come on, Mack. Come on, Molly. Let's go!"

"Push," Uncle Buddy ordered.

The horses strained, and the wagon rocked and creaked, but it wouldn't budge. Julie's sore shoulder smarted, and her arms ached from pushing so hard.

"Hold on while I take another look at that wheel," said Uncle Buddy.

Night had fallen. The humming cicadas had given way to a chorus of crickets and frogs, broken by the lonely hoot of an owl. *What if we're stranded here all night, and the wagon train leaves without us in the morning?* Julie wondered. She stole a glance at her cousin. April was chewing a fingernail. *That's exactly what I do when I'm worried*, Julie thought as the last of her hurt and anger melted away.

Julie walked over and nudged her cousin. "This is kind of like in *Little House on the Prairie* when they were trying to cross a rushing river in their covered wagon," she said. "Pa had to jump into the cold water and swim out in front of the horses to pull them across. Remember?"

April nodded. "And Laura thought they were going to drown, but they made it."

"Girls," Aunt Catherine said, handing a box down to Tracy, "we have to empty this wagon."

"Unload *all* our stuff?" April asked.

"If we lighten the load, we just might get the wagon up out of this hole."

Box by box, one suitcase after another, they lowered everything out of the wagon. The luggage, tents, coolers, and gear made a heap by the roadside.

Clip-clop, clip-clop, clip-clop.
A horse's hooves echoed over the night sounds.

"Did you hear that?" asked Tracy, shining her flashlight up and down the road. Like a ghost rider, Jimmy appeared in the small circle of light.

"Where have you guys been?" he asked. "They won't hold up the whole train for one wagon, you know. If you can't keep up, they'll leave without you in the morning."

"We're stuck!" said April. "It's not like we did it on purpose."

"Boy, are we glad to see you," said Tracy. "We need more hands to help push."

Uncle Buddy came over and handed Jimmy the end of a rope. "Maybe Hurricane can help pull us out of this hole. Here, let's run this rope from your saddle to the wagon. April, you lead Hurricane so that Jimmy can help us push."

"How far is camp?" Aunt Catherine asked.

"Twenty minutes ahead, once you crest that hill," said Jimmy, looping a half hitch around his saddle horn. He dismounted and handed Hurricane's reins to April.

"Okay, let's try it again," said Uncle Buddy after he'd tied the rope to the wagon. "One, two, three, push!"

Hurricane and the workhorses strained forward. Julie, Tracy, Jimmy, and Uncle Buddy leaned against the back of the wagon and heaved. The wagon gave one loud groan, then lurched over the rim of the pothole.

"Hooray!" the girls cheered.

"C'mon," said Tracy. "The sooner we load back up, the sooner we get to camp. I'm starving."

Aunt Catherine surveyed the pile. "Girls, this is just too much for the horses to haul up this mountain. We're going to have to make some tough choices and leave some of our things behind."

The cousins looked at one another, stunned. "Mom, we can't just—" April began to protest, but Aunt Catherine was already separating some of the pots and pans.

Tracy opened both of her suitcases and began dividing her things. Into the smaller suitcase went her Mystery Date board game, bathrobe, hair dryer, and extra sweatshirt. She picked up her pioneer dress.

"Not your dress!" said Julie. "You'll want to wear it to the big barn dance when we get to Valley Forge."

"No I won't," said Tracy, stuffing it into the suitcase with her other castoffs. "I look like a dork in that thing."

Julie wasn't about to leave *her* dress behind. But then she thought of Mack and Molly sweating and straining to pull the heavy wagon up the mountain. She thought of Laura Ingalls and the time her family moved to Kansas and had to leave even their beds and chairs and tables behind.

Pulling her suitcase from the pile, Julie lifted out her set of *Little House* books. If the soldiers at Valley Forge could go a whole winter without shoes and coats, she could do without her books. She took one last look at them and then set the books on the leave-behind pile at the side of the road.

April gasped. "Mom, don't make Julie give up her books. I'll leave my board games and my magazines and—"

"It's okay," Julie told her cousin. "I know all the stories by heart."

"But what will you do now when you're mad at me?" April asked, putting her arm around Julie.

June 21

We (finally!) made it to camp. April and I shouted as soon as we saw the wagons. April always says they look like giant loaves of Wonder Bread. She cracks me up!

Tonight the wagons were circled together around the flickering campfire. It felt like coming home.

CHAPTER
FOUR

—

MAKING HISTORY

June 28, morning

This morning we arrived in Harrisburg, the state capital. Crowds of people stood along the streets to watch and cheer as we rolled past the capitol building. I felt so proud.

We stopped at a large post office to pick up a big box of scrolls. There was a line of people still signing them as we arrived. A girl my age handed me a bunch of scrolls. She said her Girl Scout troop had been gathering signatures since Easter.

Afterward, I mailed postcards to Mom, Dad, and Ivy.

June 28, after lunch

April keeps bugging me to ride Hurricane again. She

*says whenever you fall off a horse, you have to
get right back on. I got up my nerve to feed
him an apple this morning, but no way
am I getting on his back again.*

By the time the wagon train pulled into Hershey
that night, Julie and Tracy had been on the road for two
weeks, April's family had been traveling even longer,
and everyone was looking forward to a day off.

The next morning after breakfast, April bubbled
with excitement about the theme park. Julie couldn't
wait to go on the rides, but something was nagging
at her.

"Why do I feel like I know something important
about Hershey?" she asked.

"Maybe because it's famous for Hershey bars?"
Tracy said drily.

"And Hershey's chocolate kisses—yum!" April
added.

"No, it's something else," Julie said, frowning. Then
she remembered—the night after she fell off Hurricane,
when she'd helped Uncle Buddy make a fire. The oldest
man in Pennsylvania lived in Hershey!

"Hey, April, what if we got Mr. Witherspoon
to sign one of the scrolls? He's the oldest man in
Pennsylvania—a hundred and one years old—and
he lives right here in Hershey!"

"Let's go ask Mr. Sweeney," said April. The girls
scurried around the wagons, looking for Mr. Sweeney.
They found him sitting on the back of his wagon
eating a sandwich. He greeted the girls with his
usual cheerful smile. Julie asked him about
Mr. Witherspoon.

"Ooh, yes, I read that newspaper story," said
Mr. Sweeney. "Wouldn't it be something to get his
signature on one of our scrolls? But girls, I don't
see how it's humanly possible. He lives ten miles
out of town, and there isn't time to arrange to send
somebody out there. Mr. Wescott has given the
outriders the day off." He shrugged good-naturedly
and took another bite of his sandwich. "Too bad,
though. Michigan Bob would be green with envy!"

"Who's Michigan Bob?" Julie asked.

"An old pal of mine who's collecting scrolls on
the Great Lakes route. I hear he's been bragging
since Detroit about some World Series pitcher who
signed one of his scrolls. He's hoping to be chosen to

present the scroll for President Ford to sign. The Bicentennial committee hasn't yet decided who gets to do the honors, but that signature might put me in the running!" He winked at the girls and gulped a drink from his canteen.

"Oh well, it was a good idea, anyway," said April as they strolled back to their wagon. "Hey, look, there it is—Hersheypark!" In the distance, the highest tracks of a roller coaster arched above the trees. "C'mon, let's hurry. Don't you just love roller coasters?"

Julie did love them, but somehow riding a roller coaster didn't seem as exciting—or as important—as getting Mr. Witherspoon's signature. In the back of her mind, an idea was forming. It seemed impossible, but it wouldn't go away.

"April, listen. Mr. Sweeney said it's not *humanly* possible, but what about a horse?"

"Julie, what are you talking about?" April asked without breaking her stride.

"We could ride Hurricane out to where Mr. Witherspoon lives. That way we could get his signature."

April stopped in her tracks. "What about Hersheypark?"

"I guess we'd miss it," Julie admitted. "But you can go another time, and we have theme parks in California, too. Come on, April—I can't do it by myself. Do you think Jimmy would let us borrow Hurricane? Would your parents let us go?"

April considered. "Well, I don't see why not. I can handle Hurricane like he's Lassie. I could ride in front, and you could ride double behind me, and we'd be together the whole time. But do you really want to? I thought you were afraid to get back on him."

Julie gave a weak smile. Her stomach did a somersault just thinking about her last ride and how close she had come to being trampled. Could she really muster the courage to climb back on that horse? She remembered the story Mom had once told her about her own horse, Firefly, and how she got spooked and acted crazy the time she was stung by a bee. What if Hurricane got stung, or spooked by a snake? Julie's legs turned to liquid.

But she didn't let on to April. Lightning Kelley hadn't let a raging river stop him from delivering the mail. And weren't she and April both related to him? "C'mon," Julie urged, tugging on her cousin's sleeve. "Let's go—before I lose my nerve."

❀

While Julie studied a map, April saddled up and mounted Hurricane. "Just put your foot in the stirrup and grab the saddle horn. It's easy." Julie swung up onto Hurricane's rump behind the saddle and held tight to April's waist.

"How did the pioneers ever ride horses in long dresses?" Julie wondered aloud, grateful for her blue jeans.

One nudge from April and they were off. Hurricane started out at a walk. Julie tried to relax and settle in to the rhythm.

"You okay back there?" asked April.

"I think so," Julie said nervously, trying to steady her voice. "It's kind of slippery."

"We'll take it easy, don't worry."

As they rode along, Julie felt more confident and began to enjoy the ride. But her spirits dropped when they reached the first intersection and she checked the map. "We've been riding at least half an hour and we've only gone two miles. We have eight more miles to go. We'll never make it!"

April hesitated. "Do you want to turn back?"

"No, but…what can we do?" Julie's stomach tightened. She knew the answer.

April urged Hurricane across the intersection and onto the grassy shoulder beside the road. "Let's try a nice smooth canter. You can do it. Ready?"

"Okay," said Julie in a small, shaky voice.

As soon as Hurricane took off, Julie started bouncing and sliding. "Stop!" she shouted. "I can't hold on. I'm slipping off!"

"Whoa," said April, pulling on the reins. When Hurricane came to a stop, Julie clung to April, her heart pounding.

"I have an idea," said April. "You should ride in front so that you can hold on to the saddle horn and put your feet in the stirrups. That'll make it easier for you."

"But I don't know how to steer or work the reins."

"I'll show you," said April. "It's easy."

"Stop saying it's easy!" said Julie. "It's not easy for me."

"Sorry," April said. She dismounted and helped Julie slide forward into the saddle. Then she climbed back on behind Julie and showed her how to hold the reins and guide the horse. "When you're ready to canter, lean forward a little and squeeze his sides with your heels, gently."

Swallowing her fear, Julie did as April had instructed. Hurricane sprang forward, but since Julie was already leaning forward, she kept her balance.

"Good!" April exclaimed. "That's it!"

"It feels…almost like a rocking horse, once you get used to it," said Julie. She was still gripping the horn tightly, but she no longer felt as if she were going to fall. "I think I'm getting the hang of it."

"You're doing great! I knew you could do it. You're a natural."

"I'm riding," said Julie. "I'm riding Hurricane!"

As the girls dismounted, a green station wagon flying an American flag pulled away from the curb in front of Mr. Witherspoon's house.

"Hey, that was the souvenir guy," April said. "I wonder what he's doing here."

Despite the warm summer day, Mr. Witherspoon sat on a front porch glider with a blanket over his lap. His pale blue eyes smiled at Julie from a deeply

51

lined face. "Is the Pony Express delivering my mail today?" he asked. He chuckled at his own joke, but his laugh turned into a cough.

Julie pulled Hurricane to a halt next to the man's porch. "I'm Julie and this is my cousin April. We're from the Bicentennial wagon train. But our great-great-great-grandfather really *did* ride for the Pony Express. His name was Elijah Kelley, but everyone called him Lightning Kelley."

Mr. Witherspoon squinted at them. "Lightning Kelley, eh?"

"We brought a scroll for you to sign," said April, taking it out of the saddlebag.

"It's a special scroll for the Bicentennial," Julie explained, suddenly worried. What if he didn't want to sign it? "If you sign the scroll, it means that you dedicate yourself to the ideas in the Declaration of Independence." There, that sounded impressive.

Mr. Witherspoon frowned. "You're not planning to sell this now, are you? 'Cause the fella who was just here wanted to sell my autograph for money. Even offered *me* money for it. Imagine that." The old man shook his head. "Guess he doesn't know my family's history isn't for sale."

"We'd never sell it," said Julie. "The scroll will be in a museum at Valley Forge." She offered him the clipboard with the scroll.

Mr. Witherspoon reached out a shaky hand and took it. Adjusting his glasses, he squinted at the heading. Then he looked back up at Julie and April. "You girls know about the Declaration of Independence?" Julie and April nodded. "Well here's something I bet you didn't know. *My* great-great-great-great-grandfather didn't ride for the Pony Express—but he *did* sign the Declaration of Independence."

Julie looked at April and then back at Mr. Witherspoon, her eyes round with amazement. "For real?"

Mr. Witherspoon nodded, his blue eyes crinkling into a smile. "Say, how would you girls like to see a rare copy of the Declaration that's been in my family for a hundred and fifty years?"

"We'd love to," Julie breathed.

With effort, Mr. Witherspoon got up from his porch swing. He went inside and returned carrying a slender leather tube. "My hands don't work so well anymore," he said, handing the tube to Julie.

Carefully, Julie and April opened it and slid out a delicate, tea-colored parchment. As they slowly unrolled it, Julie's eyes fell on the sacred words: *We hold these truths to be self-evident, that all men are created equal . . .*

"And there's John Hancock," said April, pointing at the first signature, with its swirling, looping flourish.

The old man pointed a crooked finger at his ancestor's name in the large cluster of signatures at the bottom. Julie leaned in closer. It was a little hard to read, but she could make it out—John Witherspoon. "Wow, he was really there in 1776. Just think—that means he knew Benjamin Franklin and Thomas Jefferson!" Julie looked up, her eyes shining. "You sure are lucky to have this."

"It was lost for many, many years," said Mr. Witherspoon. "Then one day my mother was getting an old painting framed, and there it was, hidden behind the picture."

"Thank you for showing us," said April, carefully helping Julie roll it back up and slide it into the tube.

"Now, where's that scroll of yours?" the old man asked. "Time for me to sign *my* John Hancock. Or

Mr. Witherspoon signed his name on the first line.

should I say John Witherspoon? All I need is my quill pen." He reached into his pocket.

"You have a quill pen?" Julie asked, wide-eyed.

His eyes twinkling, Mr. Witherspoon took out an ordinary ballpoint pen, working himself into another fit of laughter. He started to write, but nothing came out. "Fiddlesticks!" he said, flipping the paper over and scribbling on the back until ink came out.

"Hey, that scribble looks kind of like the loops under John Hancock's name," April remarked.

Mr. Witherspoon turned the scroll back over and signed his name on the first line. Standing on the porch, Julie gazed at his signature on the scroll and then at the tube that held the copy of the Declaration. She felt as if somehow a line had been drawn, a line from some long-ago, dusty past that connected her, today, in 1976, with the birth of the nation two hundred years ago.

June 29 (already?!)

Tracy told me I was crazy to miss Hersheypark. She said it has the best roller coaster ever and lots of FREE chocolate, too!

But riding Hurricane was way more exciting than any roller coaster. Coming home, we rode as fast as Lightning! (Get it?) And when April and I handed that scroll to Mr. Sweeney and told him how Mr. Witherspoon's great-great-great-great-grandfather had been one of the signers of the Declaration, he could hardly believe it. "Wait till Michigan Bob hears about this!" he said. "That'll put a stop to his bragging."

I think this was one of the best days of my life.

John Witherspoon

CHAPTER
FIVE

VALLEY FORGE

July 3, morning

We made it to Valley Forge!

All around us, the grassy, rolling hills look as pretty as a postcard. There's a tiny town, but most of Valley Forge is a park, with rows and rows of cannons. I wonder if they're all the way from the time of George Washington.

Huge crowds are here for the Bicentennial—Mr. Wescott says tens of thousands of people, plus hundreds of wagons. Just think of all the journeys people have taken to get here. I bet everyone has a story to tell!

Today there's a parade of all the wagons, and tonight is the barn dance. And then tomorrow is July 4, and the president will be here! I hope Dad makes it in time to see him.

Still, even with all the excitement, I'm a little sad, too, because it's the end of our trip.

❀

That evening, after a potluck supper with several other families from their wagon train, the three girls huddled inside the wagon getting ready for the barn dance.

Julie squirmed into her pioneer dress. "Do you think I should put my hair in braids, like Laura?" she asked April.

"I'd leave it loose," said April. She had on a pioneer dress, too. "Are you going to wear your bonnet?"

"Of course! Gosh, pioneers sure had to do a lot of buttons," Julie remarked.

"That's because nobody had invented the zipper yet," said Tracy, zipping up her jeans.

"Tracy, aren't you going to the dance?" April asked.

"Yeah—I'm already dressed," Tracy said, coming over to help. She fastened the top buttons on Julie's dress and tied a big bow in the sash of April's apron. "You two look so pretty," she added a bit wistfully, turning the girls around to face her.

"Too bad you left your pioneer dress behind," said Julie.

"I know," Tracy admitted. "Everybody'll be in costume tonight. I'm going to stick out like a sore thumb."

"Knock, knock," called Jimmy from outside the wagon.

"No boys allowed," said April as Tracy opened the back flap.

Jimmy looked up at Tracy, holding one hand behind his back and grinning. He was wearing a fringed buckskin jacket. His boots were shined and his hair was combed. Julie thought he looked very handsome.

"Somebody's not going to be filling up her dance card tonight," he said to Tracy, pointing at her blue jeans.

"Are *you* going to give me grief, too?" Tracy groaned, but Julie could tell she was kidding.

Jimmy gave her a taunting look. "What would you give to be able to wear that dress you left behind to the barn dance tonight?"

"Oh, let me think," said Tracy. "How 'bout a million dollars?"

"Then you owe me a million dollars," said Jimmy, calling her bluff. He held out a small bundle of cloth tied with twine. "Pay up!"

"My pioneer dress! I don't get it—how did you—?" Tracy sputtered, but Julie could tell she was pleased.

"I rescued it that night you guys got stuck up on the mountain," Jimmy told her.

"I can't believe it! Where have you been hiding it all this time—Hurricane's saddlebags?"

"Nope, my mom hid it."

"Aunt Catherine, you were in on this, too?" Tracy called.

"Guilty as charged," Aunt Catherine called back. "Now hurry and get dressed. We don't want to be late!"

"That was *so* much fun!" Julie gasped as she and April collapsed on a bale of straw. They had just learned how to square dance. It was a hot night, and the girls had worked up a sweat swinging each other to the lively fiddle music.

"I know—let's cool off by ducking for apples

again!" said April. But before they could head to the game area, Aunt Catherine cornered them.

"Time to go, buffalo gals. We've got another big day tomorrow."

"Boy, could I ever use a shower," Tracy said as the cousins walked back to their campsite. "Good thing I don't have to wear this dress again!" She twirled around, making her skirt bell out, and then linked elbows with April and spun her around. Uncle Buddy plucked a few notes on his banjo, while Julie clapped in rhythm, calling, "Swing your partner round and round!"

Suddenly, out of nowhere, Mr. Sweeney came rushing up behind them. "Julie, April—the scroll," he gasped. "It's gone."

July 3, I mean 4

We searched until after midnight, and we still can't find the scroll with Mr. Witherspoon's signature. At first, I was sure it had to be somewhere in Mr. Sweeney's wagon. But it's not, and Mr. Sweeney is convinced it was stolen!

Tracy tried to cheer me up by reminding me that

there are still more than twenty million signatures to present to the president. That's a <u>lot</u> of signatures. But are any of them from somebody whose ancestor signed the Declaration of Independence?

The next morning, Julie smelled bacon frying. *Why didn't Mom wake me up for breakfast?* she wondered sleepily. Blinking one eye open, she realized she wasn't in her bed back in San Francisco. *Pop, pop, POP!* Firecrackers . . . it was the Fourth of July . . . she was in Valley Forge, Pennsylvania, on the day of the biggest birthday celebration the country had ever seen. And Dad would be coming today! Julie felt over-the-moon happy. Jump-out-of-bed excited. Then, halfway out of her sleeping bag, she remembered—the missing scroll.

The whole campground seemed to crackle with excitement. Maybe they'd found the scroll while she was sleeping! But as soon as she saw Mr. Sweeney's face, she knew.

"We've searched everywhere," Mr. Sweeney was telling her aunt and uncle. "I have a suspicion, though. That Clark Higgins, the one who's been selling souvenirs out of his station wagon—we heard he was after that signature."

April spoke up. "Julie and I saw him that day at Mr. Witherspoon's!"

"It's wrong to sell Mr. Witherspoon's signature for money," said Julie. "I promised him it wouldn't be sold. Can't we make the souvenir guy give it back?"

Mr. Sweeney shook his head. "We would if we could find him. But Mr. Wescott ran him off again yesterday for selling without a permit."

After breakfast, Julie and April braided ribbons and wildflowers into Hurricane's mane so that he would look his best for the presentation of the scrolls to President Ford. The color guard started the ceremony with a flag raising and the Pledge of Allegiance. Everyone sang the national anthem, and then the governor of Pennsylvania took the podium to read the Declaration of Independence.

"I can't see," said Julie, standing on tiptoe and craning her neck.

"Here, sit up on Hurricane," said Jimmy. He

dismounted and handed her the reins.

"You mean it?" Julie put one foot in the stirrup, heaved herself up, and settled into the saddle. It was hard to believe that only a week ago, she'd been afraid of Hurricane.

"Make way," said April, climbing up to sit behind Julie. "Wow, what a view!"

Before them were hundreds of covered wagons that looked like ships in an ocean of people. The fifty official state wagons were fanned out in formation, flags flying.

"Here, these'll make the view even better," said Jimmy, handing April his field glasses. April took a turn and then passed them to Julie.

Julie scanned the colorful crowds. People of all ages were wearing everything from tie-dyed sundresses to cowboy chaps to Revolutionary War uniforms. Flags of all sizes flapped in the breeze.

Wait a minute. Julie trained the binoculars on a stand of trees across the field and fiddled with the focus knob. Through the leaves, she thought she saw a familiar-looking flag—familiar because it was attached to the antenna of a green station wagon.

"I'll be right back." Before April could ask

It was hard to believe that only a week ago, she'd been afraid of Hurricane.

questions, Julie slipped down off Hurricane and
began weaving her way through the crowds. She ran
as best she could, dodging horses, strollers, kids,
dogs, and Frisbees. At last she reached the station
wagon, half-hidden in a grove of trees.

"Hey!" Julie waved her arms. "Aren't you
Mr. Higgins?"

A skinny man with a mustache turned and gave
her a friendly smile. "That's me. I got hats, flags,
T-shirts, cuff links, you name it. I'm your official
Bicentennial souvenir shop."

"No you're not," said Julie. "You're not even
allowed to be here. I'm reporting you to the
wagon master."

"Now hold on just a Ben Franklin minute!"
said Mr. Higgins. "What'd I do?"

"Where is it?" Julie demanded. "The scroll with
Mr. Witherspoon's signature—the one you stole."

Mr. Higgins's head snapped back and his eyes
opened wide. Julie had to admit he looked genuinely
surprised. "For your information, missy, I got a
seller's permit to be here today." He pulled an
official-looking paper with a Bicentennial seal
from his pocket. "Go ahead—search my car if you

like. I got nothing to hide."

Julie poked her head into the back of the station wagon, but all she could see were boxes and trays of cheap souvenirs. "Well," she stammered, "then how come you're hiding under these trees?"

"A little thing called shade," said Mr. Higgins, pointing to the leafy branches overhead. "It's gonna be a scorcher today."

Julie didn't want to believe him, but she knew she couldn't prove he had stolen the scroll. She didn't feel that she had the right to search his car. Besides, if he had stolen the scroll because it was valuable, he probably had it safely stashed in a hotel room somewhere.

The president was going to arrive at any moment, and Julie didn't want to miss seeing him. She broke into a run, trying to dodge through the line of official state wagons, but a crowd of people blocked her path. In front of them, newspaper photographers were taking pictures of a man standing at the front of one of the wagons.

"Michigan Bob, what are you going to say to the president?" a reporter called.

Julie paused. "What's going on?" she asked a

young woman standing nearby.

"Didn't you hear? Michigan Bob is going to present the scrolls to the president. He has a scroll with a famous signature—"

"Oh, right, a baseball pitcher," said Julie with a nod, remembering what Mr. Sweeney had told her.

"No, this one's from some guy whose ancestor signed the Declaration of Independence," said the woman. "At least, that's what I heard."

Julie drew in a sharp breath. True, there could be many descendants of the original signers, but it was *such* a coincidence... *Something's funny about this,* she thought, frowning. She stepped away from the crowd to get a better look at the wagon. On the side of the wagon, MICHIGAN was painted in big blue letters above a picture of the Great Lakes.

There was no time to waste. Julie darted to the far end of the wagon and quickly climbed into the back. Desperately she looked around. She knew she was trespassing, but what if the missing scroll was here? It was a slim chance, just a hunch, but she had to take it. Her heart thumped wildly.

She spotted a makeshift desk covered with a jumble of papers. There they were—a whole stack of scrolls! *There must be hundreds here,* she thought. *How will I ever find it?* She picked up a pile of scrolls and began leafing through them.

"Hey—you there! What do you think you're doing?"

Startled, Julie dropped the stack of papers in her hands. "I'm sorry, I—" She bent down to gather up the mess.

"Don't touch those. Just get out." Michigan Bob had come in from the front of the wagon and was making his way toward her.

Julie stood frozen, her eyes riveted on a blank page. It was the back side of a scroll, blank except for a small squiggle of hand-drawn loops like the ones under the name John Hancock.

Julie snatched up the scroll and flipped it over. There, on the first line, was the name—*John Witherspoon.*

"Hey, gimme that," said Michigan Bob, lunging for her. But Julie was already scrambling out of the wagon. "Come back here, you!" he shouted as Julie dashed past the crowd and zigzagged across the grassy field around people and dogs, wagons and folding chairs, heading for the Pennsylvania wagon train.

Clutching the scroll close to her chest, she ran like the wind. *Like lightning,* she couldn't help thinking. *Lightning Kelley.*

Julie was breathless by the time she reached Mr. Sweeney's wagon. Holding her ribs to ease the stabbing pain in her side, she waved the scroll at him, blurting out the whole story.

"You mean to tell me that Michigan Bob stole it right out from under my nose just so he could have his fifteen minutes of fame?" said Mr. Sweeney. "Well, I'll be a star-spangled banana! And to think I considered him a friend."

Word spread like wildfire through the Pennsylvania wagon train that the missing scroll had been found. Cheering and clapping erupted as more and more people heard the good news.

Julie's relatives crowded around, hugging her and patting her on the back. Suddenly Julie felt herself wrapped in a strong pair of arms and swung into the air. "How's my girl? I hear you're a hero!"

"Dad!" Julie squealed. "You made it! I missed you so much."

Dad's long hug told her he'd missed her, too.

"And I thought you just wanted to see better,"

71

said April, starting to giggle. "I didn't know you were going to go all Nancy Drew on us!" Everybody laughed.

The wagon master came over to shake hands with Julie. "I never would have figured it out," said Mr. Wescott. "But I'm awfully glad you did."

"Will Mr. Sweeney get to present the scroll for the president to sign?" Julie asked.

"It's all taken care of," said the wagon master.

"Time out—slight change of plans," Mr. Sweeney announced. "It was Julie who saved the day." He turned to Julie, handing her the scroll. "I think it's only right that you do the honors—present the scroll for President Ford to sign, and shake his hand."

Julie turned a glowing face to Dad. "Did you hear that? I'm going to shake hands with the president!"

LOOKING BACK

AT
AMERICA'S
BICENTENNIAL

Riders on the wagon train enjoyed seeing Bicentennial decorations as they crossed the country.

The wagon train that Julie and April rode in was a real event. As planning for the Bicentennial began, people wanted special events that would inspire Americans to really think about their country's history, and what better way to do that than by traveling across the country the same way the pioneers did—by wagon train! Only this time the wagons would travel from west to east, to "bring the country back to its birthplace."

The wagon train started in early 1975, when the Pennsylvania Bicentennial Commission delivered an official state wagon to all 50 states. The wagons toured around each state, passing out the rededication scrolls. In Hawaii, people took scrolls to the outer islands by outrigger canoe, and in Alaska, the scrolls were carried by dogsled!

That summer, the first wagons began heading east. The wagons left at different times, depending on how far they had to go. Private wagons and riders traveled with the official state wagons, just as April's family did in the story. Along the way, local people helped provide meals, shelter, and water for the horses. The wagoneers faced cold weather and sickness, just as the pioneers had, but they pressed on. By spring, the wagon trains began joining together in the middle of the country. At the Missouri River, several wagon trains were loaded onto barges and floated all the way to Pittsburgh, Pennsylvania. Julie's story is set during the last leg of the journey, from Pittsburgh to Valley Forge.

Unloading the barges near Pittsburgh

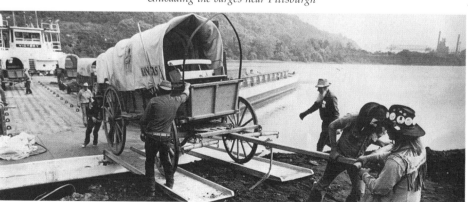

The Freedom Train

Another cross-country event was the American Freedom Train, a steam-powered locomotive that traveled around the U.S. like a moving museum of American treasures. Everywhere it stopped, families flocked to see artifacts such as Abe Lincoln's hat, Judy Garland's dress from *The Wizard of Oz*, George Washington's copy of the Constitution, and a rock from the moon. Millions more stood at the tracks and waved as the locomotive chugged past. The Freedom Train went all the way to San Francisco and parked near Ghirardelli Square, where Julie could have visited it.

On July 4, 1976, cities and towns across America threw Bicentennial picnics, parties, and parades. In Sheboygan, Wisconsin, children watched as 1,776 Frisbees went whizzing off a hill. In Ontario, California, everyone

Children rode in parades on bikes and floats.

Bicentennial quarter

ate together at a two-mile-long picnic table. Baltimore served up a 75,000-pound, 90-foot-long birthday cake in the shape of the United States. At 2:00 P.M. eastern time, bells rang all around the country to commemorate the moment when the Liberty Bell had sounded the nation's independence 200 years earlier. And families everywhere watched on TV as stately tall ships sailed up New York Harbor and fireworks exploded over Washington, D.C.

The Bicentennial did inspire Americans to think more about history—their own as well as their country's. Some gained a new interest in traditional American skills like quilting, and many families began researching their *genealogy*, or family tree. Genealogies were popular school assignments, too. One fourth-grade girl discovered that she and another boy in her class had the same English ancestor back in the 1500s!

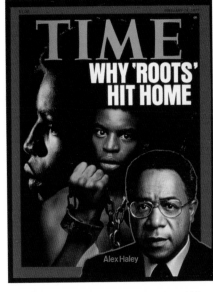

*Alex Haley's 1976 novel, **Roots**, traced his family's history from Africa to slavery in America. A best-seller, **Roots** became a TV miniseries in 1977 that broke ratings records—130 million people watched!*

Some saw the Bicentennial as a business opportunity, much like Mr. Higgins in the story. In addition to Bicentennial souvenirs, all kinds of ordinary products came with patriotic themes. You could buy a teddy bear that recited the Pledge of Allegiance or even a "Spirit of '76" coffin in red, white, and blue! Some

The Borden dairy company gave its mascot, Elsie the Cow, a colonial look for the Bicentennial.

Americans felt it was wrong to cash in on the country's birthday, which they started calling the "buy-centennial."

The "Spirit of '76" lawn tractor sold by International Harvester

And some questioned whether the nation's founding was something to celebrate at all. Native American communities in particular were divided, and some chose to commemorate Indian history and culture instead. Some people felt the nation had so many troubles that the money spent on the Bicentennial would be better spent on serious problems like poverty. Still others wondered whether Americans, so deeply divided after the wounds of Watergate and Vietnam, could come together in celebration.

The summer of 1976 proved that they could—that Americans loved their country in spite of its problems and felt connected to their fellow citizens despite their differences.

Across America, families lined the wagon train routes to cheer on the travelers and share the Bicentennial spirit.

President Ford aboard a ship in New York Harbor. To mark the nation's 200th birthday, he rang the bell 13 times—once for each of the original 13 colonies.

In his speech at Valley Forge, President Ford called this shared experience "our American adventure." He hailed the Patriots at Valley Forge and the pioneers of the American frontier for their "spirit of sacrifice and self-discipline." If Julie had really been there listening to the president that morning after her own adventure on the wagon train, she surely would have known exactly what he meant!

A SNEAK PEEK AT

CHANGES FOR
Julie

Julie is in fifth grade—and in trouble. She was only trying to help another girl in her class, but her teacher doesn't seem to care. Now Julie has to serve time in detention. Fifth grade isn't fair!

A note!

It landed on Julie's desk in the middle of social studies class. Luckily Mrs. Duncan had her back turned as she wrote lessons on the board. Julie snatched the note and hid it in the opening of her desk. Her eyes darted around the room, making sure nobody had seen the special delivery.

Mrs. Duncan was super-strict. She always wore buttoned-up blouses that pinched her neck. Even her hair was strict—starched and stiff as a ruler. She had warned the class about passing notes. "This is fifth grade, people," she'd been saying for the first few weeks of school.

As Mrs. Duncan explained about Lewis and Clark's trip through grizzly bear country toward the Rocky Mountains, Julie snuck a peek at the note. It was from Joy Jenner, who sat across the aisle from her.

Last summer, Julie had noticed a new girl walking some of the neighborhood dogs—a Chihuahua, a toy poodle, and a cute, hairy mutt—

82

at the park. Then, on the first day of fifth grade, there she was, in the same class! When Mrs. Duncan seated the class alphabetically by *first* name, Julie and Joy ended up next to each other.

A year ago, in fourth grade, Julie had been the new girl herself at Jack London Elementary, so she knew just how Joy felt. She was determined to help make Joy feel comfortable.

Julie glanced over at her new friend. Joy stopped fiddling with a strand of her reddish-brown hair. She leaned forward, her dark eyes intent on the teacher's face. Because Joy was deaf, she was trying to read Mrs. Duncan's lips, but she sometimes had difficulty understanding certain words. Julie knew Joy didn't like to ask questions in class—when she did, somebody always snickered at the funny-sounding way she talked.

Quietly, Julie opened the note. It said: *"A sack of wheat saved them?"*

Julie covered her mouth to stifle a giggle. She crossed out "sack of wheat" and wrote, *"Sac-a-ja-we-a, Lewis and Clark's Shoshone Indian guide."*

Julie tossed the note back to Joy just as Mrs. Duncan turned.

"Julie Albright, what have I said about passing notes?"

"Not to?" Julie asked.

"You and Miss Jenner have earned yourselves another demerit."

"But Mrs. Duncan, it's not what you think. Joy didn't understand—"

"No excuses." Mrs. Duncan pointed to the metal wastebasket. All eyes were on Julie as she trudged to the front of the room.

"Mrs. Duncan? The note's about our lesson," Julie said. "Honest. You can read it yourself."

"I don't want to argue. That's not how we do things in Class 5D."

Julie tried to explain further. "Joy was having some trouble reading your lips."

Joy stood and pointed to herself. In her halting, too-loud tone, she stammered, "It was my fault. Not Julie's. I passed the note."

"That's enough, both of you," Mrs. Duncan snapped. "I will not take up any more class time with this nonsense. This isn't the first time I've had to speak to you about this. You will both report to detention after school. Three o'clock sharp."

Joy looked as if she'd been stung.

"But we only have two demerits," Julie protested.

"Unless you want a whole *week* of detention, you will sit down immediately. Both of you." Mrs. Duncan pursed her lips in a thin, straight line.

Joy slumped down into the hard wooden desk chair. Julie's face flushed red and she fumed all the way back to her seat. Snickers spread through the class.

"Any of you are welcome to join them in detention," Mrs. Duncan added sharply. "Now take out your silent reading. I want fifteen minutes of quiet."

Fifth grade was no fair.

Read All of Julie's Stories,
available at bookstores and *www.americangirl.com.*

Meet Julie
Julie Albright faces big changes after her parents' divorce—
and creates some changes of her own.

Julie Tells Her Story
A school project helps Julie think about her family
in a new, more hopeful way.

Happy New Year, Julie
Julie splits her Christmas vacation between Mom and Dad.
But her whole family's invited to a Chinese New Year party.
Can they still celebrate together?

Julie and the Eagles
Julie leads an Earth Day fund-raiser, lifting hopes that
three rescued eagles can be released back into the wild.

Julie's Journey
America celebrates its 200th birthday with
an old-fashioned wagon train, and Julie is aboard
for the historic trip!

Changes for Julie
Julie runs for student body president—
against the most popular boy in school.